The Other Side

SHORTER POEMS

Also by Angela Johnson

NOVELS
Humming Whispers
Songs of Faith
Toning the Sweep

PICTURE BOOKS
The Aunt in Our House
Daddy Calls Me Man
Do Like Kyla
The Girl Who Wore Snakes
Julius
The Leaving Morning
One of Three
The Rolling Store
Shoes like Miss Alice's
Tell Me a Story, Mama
When I Am Old with You

BOARD BOOKS
Joshua by the Sea
Joshua's Night Whispers
Mama Bird, Baby Birds
Rain Feet

The Other Side

SHORTER POEMS

by Angela Johnson

ORCHARD BOOKS
NEW YORK

Orchard Books
95 Madison Avenue
New York, NY 10016

Manufactured in the United States of America
Book design by Mina Greenstein
The text of this book is set in
12 point Franklin Gothic Book.

Photographs from the private collection of
Angela Johnson

10 9 8 7 6 5 4 3 2

Library of Congress
Cataloging-in-Publication Data
Johnson, Angela.
The other side : Shorter poems /
by Angela Johnson.
p. cm.
Summary: Poems reminiscent of growing up as
an African-American girl in Shorter, Alabama.
ISBN 0-531-30114-1 (trade : alk. paper).
ISBN 0-531-33114-8 (lib. bdg. : alk. paper)
1. Afro-American girls—Alabama—Juvenile
poetry.   2. Afro-Americans—Alabama—Social
life and customs—Poetry.   3. Children's poetry,
American.   [1. Afro-Americans—Poetry.
2. Alabama—Poetry.   3. American poetry.]
I. Title.
PS3560.03712908   1998
811'.54—dc21   98-13736

To poets and Windham

CONTENTS

When I was very young and had just begun to write,
I considered myself a poet.

In my self-centered fourteen-year-old world,
poetry was immediacy
and spoke to longing, loss, hope, and absurdity.

You could not tell lies when you wrote poetry.
Poetry was sudden impact and the truth.
Poetry was odd characters in sometimes
odder circumstances.

I didn't understand meter, but
I knew what I felt and
what I saw and,
because I was very young,

when I thought myself a poet

there were no barriers. . . .

My poetry doesn't sing the song of the sonnets, but then

I sing a different kind of music—

which is what it's all about anyway.

The Other Side

SHORTER POEMS

Red Dirt

Got me some red Alabama dirt I keep

on the bathroom shelf in a heart-shaped

bottle.

Dug it up from the back of a cheap motel

in central Alabama me and Mama stayed at

when our car broke down driving south.

Was going to show it to whoever

up north.

But never have yet—can't think of anyone

who'd understand.

Still look at it and miss where I used to

wander.

Red, red dirt of Alabama.

Pullin' Shorter Down

Got the letter yesterday.

"They're pullin' Shorter down," Grandmama writes.

Some big company wanting to make a dog track.

In a few weeks we're on the road and can't get

there fast enough.

Town's coming down in a few months.

"Everybody sold out and mostly gone already," Grandmama

says in the letter and, "Come see your past before it's all

dust, baby."

I loved and hated the place.

Not enough room in the world

to tell my feelings about Shorter.

And now they're pullin' it all down.

Shorter

Got to Shorter and saw it all

from the car window.

House music blasting from the

cassette player.

Mama in a daze and not saying much

except, "Look at that," at the fields

and the boarded-up houses that just

last year I used to run in and out of.

"Can't count on much anymore."

And I think, No

you can't. . . .

Party

Carla Jackson threw me a party before I went north
last year.

Streamers, balloons, and so much food—even all the
football players couldn't eat enough food.

I danced with everybody and almost couldn't remember
anybody's name by the middle of the party.

The next morning her mom drove me to the Greyhound
in her old blue Mustang,

and me so tired.

Shorter, Alabama,

blew by in a dream.

Carla slept in the back and only woke to

see me waving from the bus window, knowing

I could never really come back.

Wash-a-Teria

Used to go to the Wash-a-Teria off the Atlanta Highway

to buy grape pop.

Women stripping their kids down to their

underwear—washing everything else.

Brown babies running 'round in their underwear

inside and throwing gravel at the gas pumps

outside.

Always was some old man in the rush rocking chair

knowing you

and you knowing him.

Everything always smelling soap clean in the hot

Alabama afternoon.

Politics

My mama's best friend in high school,

Nickie Jones, married a Republican,

had four kids, and made the FBI Most Wanted list

for something she'd done in the sixties.

Mama hid her and blamed it all on the Republicans.

Nickie stayed hidden in our house for weeks

watching *Sesame Street* with me and eating junk food.

She wouldn't let me play with my dolls 'cause she

said they were sexist.

At five I knew how to dial 911.

I almost turned her in.

Everybody in Shorter knew where she was,

and she was safe with us until

her husband showed up and somebody in Shorter

found out he was a Republican.

Nickie was mysteriously turned in.

Shorter being unforgiving of that kind of thing.

Voting

In conversation my grandmama calls them good-looking boys

standing together like that (watching TV and smiling at them),

and says it's about time those

Republicans went and sat down,

and those boys are southern too!?

She always votes, and she sure watches a lot of CNN and

C-SPAN and knows more about politics than anybody

in the family, and that's saying a lot.

She can discuss the paper from the beginning to the end.

I used to get current-event articles from her.

When somebody in the family tells her that they were nervous

about the election, she says she knew the man was in, and

my Aunt Delia said she knew too,

and I just smirk.

But then the conversation goes off about how

women in our family don't sit right

in dresses.

Grandmama

My grandmama says there's no place like Shorter
and there never will be one.
She threw a horse when she was nineteen,
right down to the ground, and always
fished on Saturdays.
She used to drag race an old Packard
with my Great-uncle Jimmy Lee and always
won.
When my mama was born she drove her
two thousand miles to see my grandaddy
in the navy.
Grandmama is fearless.
She was born in Shorter and never did
think she'd ever live anywhere else.
She says just living in Shorter would
make anybody fearless, but now that it's
being pulled down
she just looks at the old Packard and remembers.

Piano Lessons

It's hard growing up in a family that
wants you to have some talent and a little
culture.

Shorter on Saturdays was stuffed with culture.

Grandmama condemned me at eight to piano lessons.

Mama just shrugged and yawned when I asked her

to get me out of it.

Lessons with Miss Delta:

House smelled like cinnamon and dead flowers.

The first lesson I cried on the piano bench the whole time,

with Miss Delta feeding me cookies.

Tried the second lesson and we both cried.

Miss Delta cried into sweet-smelling handkerchiefs,

and I wiped my nose on my white blouse.

Mama showed up, looked at both of us,

then dragged me forever away from culture in Shorter.

Death Chest

Last year, in the last field out of Shorter,

me and Donna Anderson used to skip school and hunt

for things to put in her death chest.

She'd been keeping the chest

(her Uncle Bobby's army footlocker)

since we were in the first grade.

She'd lost a pet then,

Homer the frog.

She kept diaries, old letters tied with ribbon,

dried butterflies in gauze, and cotton doilies

stolen from her grandmama's tables in the chest.

Donna figured it was best to be ready for anything.

Homer was the first thing in the chest.

"That girl's crazy," Mama would moan.

Donna always gave me the key when she

went on vacation in case she was smashed by a

runaway bumper car at Six Flags,

or drowned in the hotel bathroom by a mad maid.

I appreciated Donna for her romantic ways,

but never had the nerve to get my own death chest.

I always lock the bathroom doors in hotels though.

Ghost Houses

Already tearing down some of the old houses.

Couldn't be that much power in the whole world.

They were too solid, too whole.

Soon there would be no Grandmama's house.

Driving through Shorter. . .

Remembering the red dusty days sitting on the porch.

Watching it all go by.

No more porches now.

Too many ghosts.

No more Shorter.

Hiding Place

Yesterday found the old shack by Line Creek
that hid me for a whole afternoon when I was seven.

Ran away when my dog died.

Uncle Jack having to shoot it after it got hit.

No vets in Shorter then.

No doctors, dentists, or drugstores either.

The shack might be the only thing that

stays standing in Shorter, but I can't hide

there anymore.

Looked at it for a while, then passed it up

to face the reality of Shorter.

War

Every day after school I used to run into town to listen

to Harper Crew as he leaned back on his chair

by Miss Sally Hirt's store and talked about war.

All kinds of war.

Wars with bombs.

Wars with swords.

Even wars with aliens.

Always told the same stories, and I listened

as they scared me to death

and made me sad.

One day Harper didn't show up.

Word was he got sent to the state hospital

after breaking all the windows at an army recruiting

office up in Birmingham.

Miss Annie Morgan

I waved to Miss Annie Morgan this morning.

She lived in Shorter all her life and most of the

time sat on her porch and smoked a pipe.

The only person she'd speak to in the whole town

was my grandaddy.

Grandaddy said Miss Annie used to own a dance club

and would dress in silk dresses and red lipstick.

She'd dance down the red dirt roads of Shorter—heels

and all.

Once she gave me an old dress to play in.

She'd given the others to the Baptist Church years ago

after being saved.

Some say she'd killed somebody.

But Grandaddy said that was just Shorter country talk,

and people just didn't like folks who

could care less about them.

That's why I waved at Miss Annie.

Working the Roots

Secretly, it was said, my great-great-grandmama, who looked
just like me, was a root worker.

A voodoo woman who knew potions.

All kinds.

She could find you your true love,

and get rid of someone you didn't want to love you.

Feared by all, she'd stand on her porch,

right on the Shorter border,

and feed her chickens.

They'd been alive, some say, for about twenty-five years,

and none had ever died.

One day my great-great-grandmama got sick and couldn't

feed her chickens.

They all died the next day.

Lying in her flower beds, drawing red ants and flies,

'cause no family or neighbors had the nerve to touch 'em.

Looks

I stood on the curve in the road by my grandmama's

house last night

in my Docs and a Twirl-the-World T-shirt,

thinking about looks.

My locks itched the back of my neck

and my striped shorts flapped around my legs

in the soft Alabama breeze,

and I wondered if my whole being

would stop here,

on this

road and this place

if nothing else of this town

existed.

Horses

Mr. John Jacobs used to sit me on the old carousel

horse outside his Aunt Sally's store.

The old horse was black with a red saddle,

and for the few minutes you sat on him he

took you across the sky and over the world.

The rest of the horses lived in the old storage

building in the back.

Saw 'em all being loaded up in a truck standing

on the Atlanta Highway about sundown.

My horse was the last one they loaded up.

Mr. John just watched and kicked dirt as

the old horse was loaded up with the rest.

We both stared as the truck drifted down

the road, past the field of kudzu.

And I wondered if he'd ever fly again.

Smoking with T. Fanny

T. Fanny moved in next door to us when I was eight.

Me and T. Fanny hung around too much together, Mama said.

Got caught smoking cigarettes with T. Fanny in the old

McAllister house.

Cigarettes we'd taken from her cousin Carl who didn't

have much sense.

He couldn't understand what all the fuss was about—

he'd started when he was nine.

My grandmama found out and stuck me and T. Fanny

in the broom closet with a pack of smokes,

unfiltered, and said, "Go to it."

We never did smoke again,

but T. Fanny sends my grandmama a carton of unfiltered

cigarettes on her birthday every year.

The Other Side

I used to stand on top of the shed in the back of my
grandmama's house and see the other side.
The other side of where I was.
The other side had tall buildings and I could buy
hot dogs and pretzels on the street.
At night the hum of the subway and faraway sirens
would put me to sleep.
I dreamed of the other side.
I'd seen it on vacation and TV.
The other side didn't have a creek or magnolia trees
and warm women who smelled like cookies hugging you
on hot, sticky Sunday afternoons.

If I stood for a long time,
the other side would fade and
where I stood would light my world.

Dancing in the Moonlight

Me and Kesha Cousins used to dance to hip-hop music
in the woods.

Boom box blasting through the trees.

We had to do it in the woods 'cause her parents
got saved and didn't allow it.

Kesha just wanted to dance.

In a video maybe one day, she said.

Figured she could still get in heaven if dancing was
her only sin.

Kesha met a boy at the revival in Waugh,
then we stopped dancing in the moonlight.

Next time I saw her she was slipping
out of the Blue and Gray Club in high heels.

I guess she figured after she'd sinned
more than once heaven was closed to her.

The New House

Two years before we moved to Ohio

we moved out of Grandmama's house

to our own about a mile up the road.

I didn't come out of the house for

half the summer, mad at Mama. . . .

Mama not knowing what to do

shipped me off to my cousins in

Diamond, Ohio.

Diamond in late July being

hot like southern Alabama;

made it better.

I rode bikes, picked blackberries,

and fell in love with a boy whose

name I've already forgot.

Played strip poker with my cousins,

and laughed till I cried.

And never once thought that much

about how sad I really was,

until I was almost in Tennessee

looking out the bus window

and not going back to Grandmama's house.

Walter

Me and Walter used to go skinny-dipping

down by Line Creek

and pick plums and throw them onto the Atlanta Highway.

Walter wanted to live in the city, but there

was nothing to tell him

that's where he'd end up.

The only thing Walter liked in Macon County

was his mama and me,

and I got this picture

of me and him in diapers

eating pudding.

When his mama died he started throwing

the plums and anything he could find

in Line Creek.

Before the county got him,

somebody said they saw him get in a

car off the Atlanta Highway.

I walked the road two weeks looking. . . .

When I left Shorter, I put a note

in the plum tree for Walter.

Cried yesterday when Mr. Clyde Cole's pickup

hauled away the last

of me and Walter from the creek.

Crazy

You'd have to be

crazy

to want to live

your life in

a place like Shorter, Alabama.

The heat,

the red ants, and

twenty miles to

any mall.

You'd have to be crazy

to want to live

in a place where

every other person is

related to you

and thinks they know

everything about your

life.

You'd have to be crazy

to want to wake

up every morning to sweet

magnolia and moist red

dirt.

You'd have to be

crazy.

Sirens

Red lights in the cold night

is what I remember.

You could crack the ice

in the puddle by the

front door, and I did.

I remember looking for

more puddles

and ice,

until I couldn't feel my

bare feet,

and some woman

who smelled of sweet talcum

hugged me to her

and rubbed them.

Didn't know it could

get that cold in Alabama.

When the sirens took

my daddy away forever (the doctors will help him, baby)

I thought I'd

never be warm again.

Counters

My Uncle Fred has a slash

across his face from

some redneck

trying to

stop him from ordering

a lemonade from a lunch counter

in Montgomery.

When the weather changes, it

aches him, he says,

but smiles when

he says it, whenever he says it.

All my mama could remember

was how Grandmama had

screamed and

talked about

leaving the South.

All I can think is

how terrible it was

and how beautiful

it made him.

Into the Light

There is a picture of
my mama from 1973
in a faded T-shirt that
says BE A HUMAN BEAN.
Too skinny, wearing raggedy
tennis shoes, and
squinting into the hot
Macon County sun.

Grandmama noticed that she
seemed not to breathe
when she was still.
Her ribs showed and she
looked like an ebony doll.
At night she'd sit on the
side of the bed and put
her hand on my mama's back

and feel the life run

through her.

I think of my mother's eyes in the sun

as we drive back into Shorter.

Later, when we are at Grandmama's,

she takes her hand off my back,

covers me,

and tips out of

my dark room into

the light.

On the Steps

Had never seen a crack pipe till

we moved to Ohio,

and I found one on the

steps to our apartment.

Mama packed us up in the middle of the night

and drove right up

to the freeway.

Sitting by the on-ramp all night long.

Playing Sam Cooke music

till the sun came

over Lake Erie.

Shaking her head and

looking at me.

Saying she was ashamed we

all couldn't do any better.

Gettin' Old

One day I figured I'd get old,

real old like Mr. Crawford Fisher

(who'd lived in Shorter forever

and always gave us a cold

drink when we passed his house).

But T. Fanny said, "No way. Nobody is that old."

So on some days I'd spy on Mr. Fisher,

and wonder,

just how he could get to be so old.

Got up enough nerve to ask Mr. Fisher one day

what his secret was,

Mama figuring he had to be at least one hundred.

He said he didn't know 'cause he

didn't know anybody as old as he was.

T. Fanny said, "See?"

Miss Pearl

She told immigrant stories,

and talked about growing up in

Jamaica when she got sad.

She stayed clear of heavy traffic,

and walked down the dirt back roads

after the sun went down.

Miss Pearl would cook all day long,

and stay up all night

feeding me and Walter jerk chicken.

She says leaving Shorter is

like leaving Jamaica

and her family again.

She says she'll move to Atlanta

to live with her grandniece.

But she'll miss the dirt roads.

And when I tell her

she might like the city,

she asks me if I do.

But instead I tell her about growing

up in Shorter.

War II

My daddy had Vietnam dreams.

Nightmares that used

to rip him out of bed screaming

and running into the living room.

Helicopters machine-gunned

down on him, and he

used to yell that he couldn't

get the blood off.

And near the end I didn't even

wake up anymore.

I didn't hear Mama saying,

"Baby, baby, baby."

And I couldn't hear him crying.

So at the end I was almost

deaf,

and the silence wrapped

me up warm.

And I didn't know it,

but that war in the jungle

had followed my daddy all the way

to Shorter.

Country Girl

Had this cousin that was a Black
Panther, who left and came back
to Shorter before I was born.
And nobody knew what to make
of her.
Her mama tried to get her
to wear a girdle,
and she got in a fight
at the Esso station in Waugh
and the Blue and Gray Club in Tuskegee.
She'd smoke bud
by her mama's chicken coop,
and could stare down
a killer (Mama's words).
But she used to make
the best biscuits in the world
and would fish all day with her daddy.

And none of the family could understand

how somebody who

could act like a country girl

could be mad as hell with the world.

Nineties

Had to leave the South

to hear somebody call me a nigger

for the first time.

Had to have my head

out the window in

a west side neighborhood

in Cleveland

to hear a girl about my age

scream that knifing word

at my mama's car.

Had to make Mama stop

so I could look at the

face of somebody who

dressed just like me

and probably

wanted what I did

from the world,

but would never live in

mine.

Where You Been

Grandmama says

when the last of Shorter is gone,

everybody's gonna talk what's left of it

all to the

ground.

And they're gonna say

it's not where we've been

but where we're going,

and that would be a lie.

We've been away

and come back.

We lived in back of the woods

and moved to town.

We've died in wars

and sometimes waited for

the wars to come home to kill us.

She looks at me,

and wipes her face

with a lace handkerchief,

and I know the world is a

whole lot different when you're

fourteen and leaving,

finally leaving,

the red, red dirt of Alabama.